This book belongs to

....

....

....

For Ferdinand - JE
For Elinor, my friend who loves leaves! - CJC

© 2009 The Chicken House

First published in the United Kingdom in 2009 by
The Chicken House, 2 Palmer Street, Frome, Somerset, BA11 1DS
www.doublecluck.com

Text © 2009 Jonathan Emmett
Illustrations © 2009 Caroline Jayne Church

Designed by Ian Butterworth

Find out more about Jonathan Emmett's books at
www.scribblestreet.co.uk

Printed and bound in China

1 3 5 7 9 10 8 6 4 2

British Library Cataloguing in Publication Data available
Library of Congress Cataloguing in Publication data available

HB ISBN: 978-1-904442-99-8-
PB ISBN: 978-1-906427-23-8

Leaf Trouble

Jonathan Emmett

Illustrated by

Caroline Jayne Church

Chicken House

A fresh breeze blew across
the woodland, tickling the
tall grass and trembling
the trees. Summer had left
and autumn had arrived.

Pip Squirrel stuck his head out
of the nest and sniffed the air.

'Something's changed!' he decided.
And he scampered off to find out
what it was.

Pip's nest was in an old oak tree.
Pip loved the old tree and he knew
every bit of it from twig to trunk.

But something was happening to the tree.
It was happening so slowly that Pip
hadn't noticed it – until now.

He skittered to a stop and stared
at the leaves beside him.

He was so
surprised
that he
let go.

'Wwwaaaahhhh!'

squealed Pip as he tumbled down
through the branches
and landed – **'OOOOFFFF!'** –
on the woodland floor.

OOOOFFFF!

Pip lay there for a moment staring up at the
leaves. 'They've changed colour!' he gasped.

And he was right. The last time Pip
had looked closely at the leaves,
they had all been GREEN –
but now there were lots of colours,
YELLOW and ORANGE
and even RED!

As Pip watched, one of the leaves

dropped off

and

drifted

down,

towards

the

ground.

He jumped up and ran after it
and caught it in his paws.
But even as he got to it,
another leaf began to fall.

Pip ran after the second leaf
and just managed to catch it
before it hit the woodland floor.
'Not again!' gasped Pip, as a
third leaf began to fall.

Pip was still racing around
trying to catch the falling leaves
when his sister, Blossom,
scurried up.

'Good,' panted Pip. 'You're just in time.'

'Just in time for what?' asked Blossom.

'To help save the tree, of course,'
puffed Pip. 'It's falling to pieces.'

'But that's been happening for days,'
said Blossom, pointing to the leaf-covered ground.

'Then we must stop it NOW!' insisted Pip.

Pip and Blossom collected all
the fallen leaves into a big heap.

'Now what?' asked Blossom.
'We put them back, of course,'
said Pip.

So Blossom carried the leaves up
into the tree, where Pip tried to
stick them back onto the branches.
But it didn't work very well.

Then – all of a sudden – there was a
HUGE gust of wind and HUNDREDS OF
LEAVES began to fall! Pip and Blossom
were chasing around frantically,
trying to gather them, when
Mum Squirrel arrived.

'What ARE you two up to?'
she asked.

When Mum found out what
Pip and Blossom had been doing,
she couldn't help smiling.

'But Pip,' she said,
'the tree has to lose its leaves.'

And she explained that looking
after the leaves was hard work for
the tree and that, after keeping them all
summer, it needed to rest for a while.

'But I love this tree,' said Pip, sadly. 'It's our home. And I want it back the way it was!'

'It will be,' said Mum. 'When spring comes, the leaves will all come back again. They've only gone for a while.'

'Like when the sun sets and then comes back again?' said Pip.

'Like when the sun sets,' agreed Mum, 'only the leaves will take a little longer to come back.'

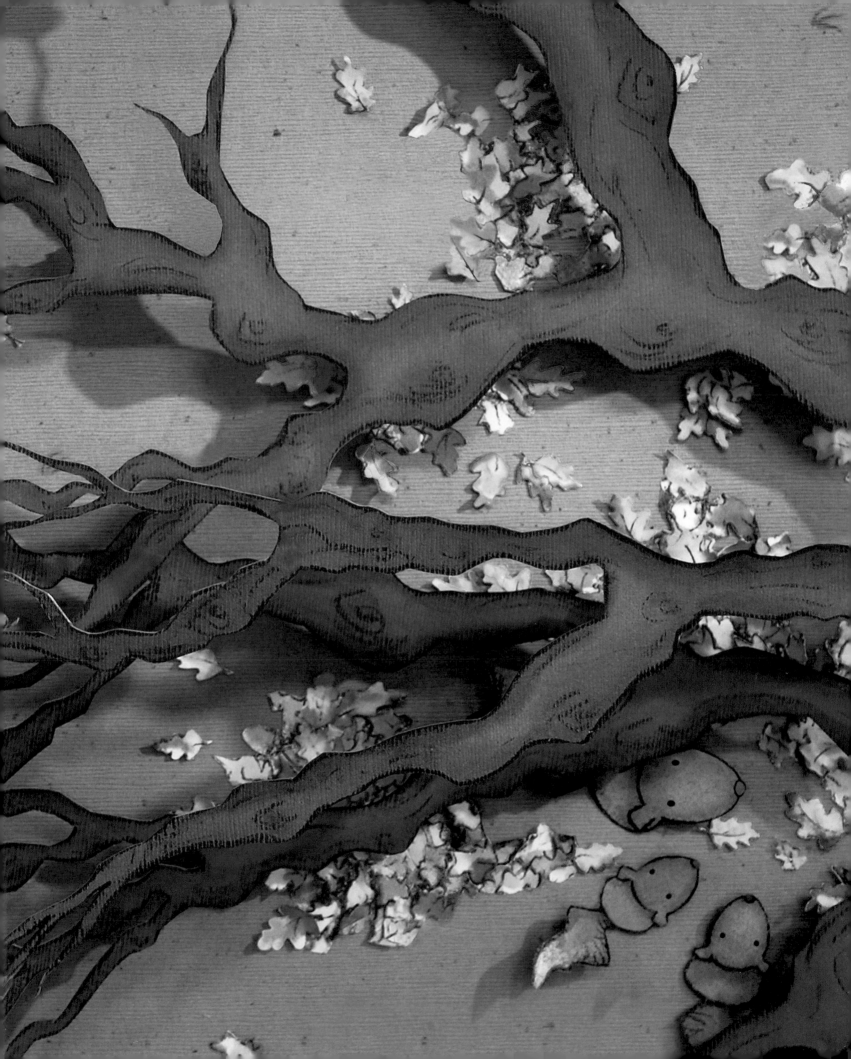

Pip, Blossom and Mum played beneath
the old oak tree until sunset.

Before they left they collected some leaves to take back to their

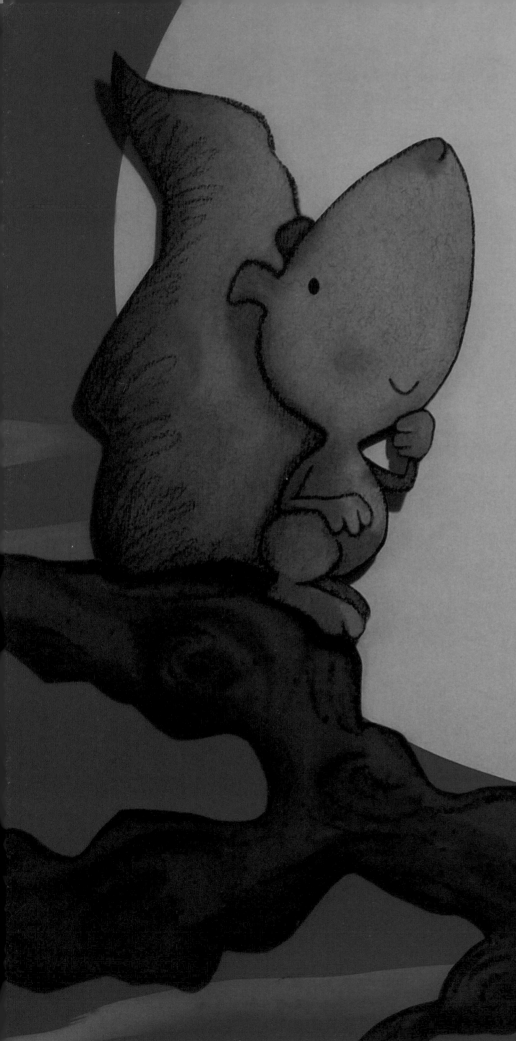

'They're such beautiful colours,' said Pip, smiling. 'And now I understand why.' He held up a pawful of leaves to show them.

'They're the colours of the sunset,' said Pip.